THE LOUGH NEAGH
MONSTER

Noblett lives in Lough Neagh.
One day he receives a visit from his
wild and troublesome cousin
Nessie, from Scotland.
But the two monsters do not see
eye-to-eye!

'Sam McBratney writes with a refreshingly individual
style; his characters, both children and adults,
are clear and convincing'
TIMES LITERARY SUPPLEMENT

'One of the most perceptive writers
for young people'
THE GUARDIAN

SAM McBRATNEY, a former schoolteacher, is the author of numerous award-winning books for children. One of his best-known and most-loved books, *Guess How Much I Love You?*, has been translated into many different languages and has been a bestseller in many different countries. His book *Put a Saddle on the Pig* won the Bisto Book of the Year Award in 1993, while *The Chieftain's Daughter* scooped the Bisto Book of the Year Merit Award the following year. McBratney lives in Glenavy, County Antrim. He is married, with three grown-up children, and an ancient tortoise!

OTHER SAM McBRATNEY BOOKS FROM THE O'BRIEN PRESS

Art, You're Magic
The Chieftain's Daughter
Guess How Much I Love You?

SAM McBRATNEY

Illustrations DONALD TESKEY

THE O'BRIEN PRESS
DUBLIN

First published 1994 by The O'Brien Press Ltd,
20 Victoria Road, Dublin 6, Ireland.
Tel: +353 1 4923333; Fax: +353 1 4922777
E-mail: books@obrien.ie
Website: www.obrien.ie
Reprinted 1997, 1999, 2003.

ISBN 0-86278-375-5

British Library Cataloguing-in-Publication Data
McBratney, Sam
The Lough Neagh Monster
I. Title II. Teskey, Donald
823.914 [J]

4 5 6 7 8 9 10
03 04 05 06 07 08

Typesetting, layout, editing, design: The O'Brien Press Ltd
Printing: Cox & Wyman Ltd

1

There are good monsters, there are monsters who are not so good, and there are monsters who are *downright pests.*

Everybody knows that the Loch Ness monster is a downright pest.

She has been annoying people for years and years. She likes nothing better than headbutting boats or frightening old-age pensioners wrapped up in their tartan rugs. And she would be a far worse pest if she wasn't afraid of one thing: she's afraid that they'll capture her one day and put her in an underwater zoo – as if she were a dolphin or an oversized goldfish. If you ever see the Loch Ness monster, just say that word to her: 'Zoo.' You won't see her for dust.

One day last summer, Nessie went too far with her nonsense. In the morning she was spotted chasing cows across muddy fields – a thing she loves to do. In the afternoon she

pulled three fishermen off the rocks and into the water – just for fun. In the evening she took a bite out of a yacht, then finished off a splendid day by creeping ashore and eating a line of washing.

Now, people are bound to talk about you if you behave like that. Needless to say, Loch Ness was soon full of folk armed with cameras. Scientists came with sonar equipment and underwater probes, and journalists arrived with sharpened pencils and laptop computers.

Nessie, who was no fool, could tell that these people meant business. And that night she had a terrifying dream about an underwater zoo.

'You'd better lie low for a while, Nessie old girl,' she said to herself. 'How boring! Or maybe you could take a holiday. I think it's time you paid a visit to that cousin of yours who lives in Lough Neagh.'

2

You will find Lough Neagh quite
easily on the map of Ireland. It is at
the top right-hand side, in the middle
of the province of Ulster, and you
will certainly see it if you look out of
the window as you come in to land
at Belfast International Airport.

On a wild day it has waves as high
as walls. On a quiet day it lies like a
jewel under the ever-changing sky.
Lough Neagh is vast and beautiful;
there could be no finer home for a
huge beast than this place, the largest
inland water in all of Europe.

Why, then, have we never heard of the Lough Neagh monster?

Well, think of the differences within families. One child is loud and noisy, the other is shy. One is clever at sums and music, the other is good with her hands and never has her nose out of a book. They are not the same.

And so it is with monsters. They are not all the same. The monster in Lough Neagh never ate washing or scared old people wrapped up in their car rugs. And, by the way, he never had bad dreams about an underwater zoo, because he knew that hardly anyone had the faintest idea that he even existed. This was exactly how Noblett, the Lough Neagh monster, wanted things to be: peaceful and quiet.

Then one day he returned to his cave to find that he had a visitor.

'Hello there, Nobby, my old dodo,' said a familiar voice, 'how are you keeping? It's me – are you pleased? It must be, oh, a hundred years since I saw you last.'

It *was* a hundred years, but they seemed like only yesterday to Noblett. On that last visit his wild cousin Nessie had eaten a whole thatched roof in County Tyrone and caused him no end of trouble.

'What do you want?' he said.

'Don't you think we should keep in touch, for goodness sake,' said Nessie, settling herself on the only bed. (She did not reveal that half of Scotland was looking for her with cameras and underwater probes.) 'You don't mind if I sleep here, do you, Nobby? It's such a long swim to your place, you've no idea. And then in the morning – we'll get up and have ourselves some *fun*. Aren't you pleased?'

Poor Noblett closed his eyes as he leaned against the wall of his cave, but not because he was tired. He was trying to stop thinking about that word 'fun'.

Please let it rain, he thought. There'll be nobody about and they won't see her and she'll get bored stiff and she'll go back home. Let it rain and rain and let the north wind blow.

3

It was a beautiful morning.

Nessie woke after a night of thrilling dreams in which she ate a whole thatched roof and towed a fishing boat miles from where it wanted to go.

'Come along, Nobby,' she cried, 'anyone would think you were ancient. Back home I always beat the sun out of bed.'

'I'm amazed you even sleep,' mumbled Noblett, who was not brimming over with happiness.

This was going to be a long day.

Sure enough, by mid-morning the 'fun' had started. Nessie suddenly

appeared before Noblett with a look of mad glee in her eyes and a stick in her mouth.

The stick was an oar.

'Where did you get that?'

'Up there,' said Nessie, pointing with her tail.

Noblett risked a peep above the water.

He saw two terrified people huddled together in a small boat. Anyone could tell that they'd just had the shock of their lives.

'Did they get a look at you?' Noblett asked angrily. 'What do you want an oar *for*, anyway?'

'You needn't be such a jealous old dodo, Nobby, go and get the other one. They had two oars.'

'I don't *want* an oar!' snapped Noblett. 'Come on, we'd better get out of here quick.'

4

With a flick of his flippers and a flash
of his fins Noblett headed towards
the middle of the lough where the
water was deep and cold; but he had
to stop and come back again. Nessie
didn't follow him. She had just
spotted twenty or thirty windsurfers
having a wonderful time close to the
shore.

'Yipee,' she yelled, and did an
underwater somersault. Then she
went wild altogether.

It is sometimes said of people who are on their holidays that they 'let their hair down'. This means that they are prepared to do things, often quite silly things, that they wouldn't do back home. Nessie, of course, was quite prepared to do silly things back home, but now she was ready for even worse mischief. She suddenly stuck up her head like a periscope in the middle of the windsurfers and blew a spurt of water over their heads!

Every single one of the surfers lost their grip. Their sails dipped and they all flopped into the water.

Then Nessie popped up her tail. Then she allowed her long body to form hoops on the water as if she were doing an impression of a bridge with arches.

The surfers threshed around and screamed for help at the tops of their voices.

Noblett groaned in desperation. This was awful! This was worse than last time. Maybe I could tie her up or something, he thought.

At teatime Nessie wandered ashore and found herself in the playground of a school. Luckily the children had all gone home, and so had the workmen who were working on the road nearby. After hanging a wheelbarrow up a tree, Nessie

scratched her back on the bicycle
sheds and left a trail of monster
prints across some newly-laid

cement. She also tried to speak to a very peculiar yellow creature, but it seemed to be dead.

And there was more to come before bedtime. Failing to find cows, Nessie chased some sheep. Then she ate a

line of washing on the shore of County Armagh and a barnful of bales near Toomebridge.

Her poor cousin was a nervous wreck, but Nessie slept sweetly all night.

5

'I do not approve of your behaviour yesterday,' Noblett said frankly to his cousin at breakfast time. 'It was unspeakable, gratuitous and self-indulgent.'

'Don't be such a grumpy old bore,' replied Nessie, annoyed that she didn't know what those big words meant. 'I thought you'd be pleased to have a little fun.'

'Look! People know when their washing is missing, they're not

stupid! They know when their hay
bales have been eaten. When they
look up and see wheelbarrows
growing on trees they are going to

come looking for us. And times have changed, you know. If they can put people on the moon it won't be long before they can find a couple of monsters at the bottom of a lake! Your behaviour is gratuitous, self-indulgent and dangerous to our whole way of life!'

This was a powerful speech – impressive, even. For just a moment Nessie had a vision of an underwater zoo, complete with iron bars.

'All right, Nobby, today we'll do what *you* want to do. I mean, do you ever do anything interesting?'

'Of course I do,' said Noblett.
'Come with me and I'll show you.
This will certainly take your mind off
chasing cows and sheep.'

Well well well, thought Nessie as she cruised along at monster speed, perhaps old Nobby isn't such a dodo after all. What can this exciting thing be?

It didn't take long to get there. After some minutes Noblett stopped in the middle of nowhere, and said, 'Here we are.'

For as far as the eye could see, rays of ghostly sunlight fell upon row after row of carefully tended plants. Some of these plants, the tallest ones, wafted backwards and forwards in gentle currents as they reached upwards for the light. Here and there among the plants there rose up

tunnels and towers of stone and carefully crafted bridges. Through the whole arrangement swam a happy population of eels and fish.

'Is that *it?*' said Nessie. 'This is what you *do* all day?'

'Not all day and not every day,' said Noblett proudly, 'but yes – I am a gardener. And I build things. Watch where you put your tail, please.'

Nessie was speechless. How boring could you get? Could this gardening ever be as much fun as playing peek-a-boo with a boatload of tourists? No. Never.

Or could it! All of a sudden a wonderful thought came into her head. Maybe this gardening had possibilities. Maybe, after all, it could be *fun*.

6

It wasn't long before the headlines began.

IS THERE A PLESIOSAUR
IN LOUGH NEAGH?
asked the *Irish Times*.

A DINOSAUR CHEWED MY OAR,
SAYS BOATMAN
wrote the *Belfast Telegraph*.

WINDSURFER SEES SEVEN MONSTERS
DOING SYNCHRONISED SWIMMING
reported the *Independent*.

People began to take notice.
Officials in the tourist board licked
their lips and thought about flocks of
American tourists.

Fishermen worried that Lough Neagh's famous eels would all be eaten.

In the little primary school of Ballymascullion the excitement rapidly became unbearable, for this was the school, you remember, where Nessie had hung the wheelbarrow up the tree and walked in wet cement.

The children of Ballymascullion had never worked so hard. They wrote about monsters and talked about monsters and created monsters using clay, *papier maché* and computer graphics. Their teacher, Mr Livingston, was worse than his pupils, for he was mad about monsters and always had been. In his bookcase there were over one hundred books about dinosaurs and ancient reptiles. Not only could he say 'plateosaurus' and 'plesiosaurus' as easily as you or I might say 'cup and saucer', but he could also talk for an hour or more about the differences between those creatures.

Teachers are best at teaching what they are interested in, and so the children of Ballymascullion school knew more about dinosaurs than any other class in Ireland.

Mr Livingston was a little late on Wednesday morning. As soon as he arrived, all his children began to shout out the incredible news with one voice:

'Mr Livingston, Mr Livingston, it's been back, it's been back.'

'Calm yourselves down, said Mr Livingston sternly. 'Now, one at a time. Speak, Caroline MacIlhagga.'

'Mr Livingston, one of our bicycle sheds has been taken there were two

yesterday and now there's only one
and the other one has *gone!*'

Mr Livingston ran outside to see for
himself. By jove. The thing really was
gone.

'Maybe the wind blew it away,'
Nicholas Titterington piped up. The
storm of abuse from the rest of the
class nearly blew him away.

'Maybe the wind blew the
wheelbarrow up a tree!' cried
Caroline MacIlhagga.

'Maybe the wind left its prints in the
cement!' said her brother Michael.

'Quiet!' roared Mr Livingston. 'We need to think. If this is the work of the Lough Neagh plesiosaur, we must all keep a clear head!'

He forgot to mark the roll. He forgot to take in homework.

'Children,' said Mr Livingston, 'maths are cancelled. There will be no English today. Or geography or history. And you can forget RE and PE as well – we are having craft, design and technology all day.'

A few hoorays occurred. Then: 'What are we making, Mr Livingston?'

'We are making a trap. A big trap. Children, if the Lough Neagh plesiosaur visits us once more, then let us not be unprepared!'

7

Meanwhile, somewhere in Lough Neagh, Noblett had no idea that things were stirring in the outer world. Indeed, he was feeling quite pleased with himself for pointing out to Nessie that this was *his* patch, and that she'd better behave herself.

That was the moment when Nessie drifted down from the surface carrying something rather large.

'I brought you this for your garden, Nobby,' she said. 'It's a sort of tunnel – you know, one of those things for fish to swim in and out of. Are you pleased?'

This wasn't a tunnel, of course, it was a bicycle shed. A stolen bicycle shed. Noblett's great slow-beating heart sank, for somebody somewhere was bound to notice that it was missing.

'You don't seem very pleased, Nobby. In fact you've got your dodo face on again. If you don't like my present why don't you just say so?'

Noblett did say so. There was an awful row. He called her an ungrateful reptile and she called him a boring old gardener and *he* said she would end up in an underwater zoo and *she* howled that he had an ugly warty face and crooked flippers.

'And you'll take that bicycle shed back where it belongs!' roared Noblett.

'All right then,' said Nessie, suddenly as nice as could be. She was amazed to find that her cousin

had a temper even worse than her own, and besides, she didn't care two hoots what happened to the bicycle shed.

'We'll take it back in the morning if you like, Nobby. Will that please you?'

The bicycle shed might look ever so nice up a tree, she was thinking.

8

It's not every day that you see a monster walk out of the water carrying a bicycle shed.

Did the children of Ballymascullion run away screaming with terror? Not at all. They were monster experts. Here are some of the things they said:

'Oooo, he's a really big plesiosaur.'

'Or a plateosaur.'

'He might be a *she*, don't forget.'

'I think he or she is a diplodocus reticulata.'

'No way, look at the hinged hip-joints.'

Even Nicholas Titterington, who couldn't tell a full stop from a

decimal point, shook his head wisely
and said, 'It must have over seventy
cervical vertebrae in that neck, you
know.'

Unlike his children, Mr Livingston
seemed to be affected by something
rather like stage-fright as the great
beast lumbered ashore. He might
have been a stone-age hunter staring
up at a skyscraper.

'Sir, shall we activate ART?' called
Caroline MacIlhagga.

ART (short for Ancient Reptile Trap)
had been designed by Caroline and
her brother Michael, the two most
intelligent people in the class
(including Mr Livingston). Everybody

knew that the MacIlhaggas would end up at university later in life. Like most people who make traps, they had absolute faith in it. ART couldn't fail.

There were three parts to ART – or, to put it another way, the children were organised into three gangs: first, the rubber tyre gang. Their job was to let loose fourteen rubber tyres, on ropes, so that these would hang down from the trees like a forest of large black polo mints, thus throwing the creature off-balance.

Then the second group would attack with the assault net (one of those used by the army to camouflage tanks). Finally, the tent peg gang would run forward and peg the net, with its struggling contents, to the ground. The Lough Neagh plesiosaur could no more escape than a sack of potatoes.

'Shall we activate ART, Mr Livingston?' Caroline called again. And when no answer came, she yelled: 'GO WITH THE TYRES!'

It rained down rubber tyres. The monster tried to eat one and may have hurt a tooth, for a sound came out of it like a wounded trumpet. Its tail fairly whistled through the air and thumped into the wall of the school.

The wall fell down. Nicholas

Titterington gasped. 'Mr Livingston, that monster knocked a big hole in our *school.*'

'Never mind, boy, we needed a new one anyway,' cried Mr Livingston, who was back to normal again. 'Throw the net. Quick, the net, the net!'

The gang attacked, bravely led by Michael MacIlhagga. They were followed by the tent peg gang. By now the din was so awful that no-one heard Caroline screaming with rage: 'You've captured the BICYCLE SHED, you stupid fools!'

True, the prisoner in the net was the bicycle shed, not the monster, which was on its way to the water, trailing half-a-dozen rubber tyres behind it.

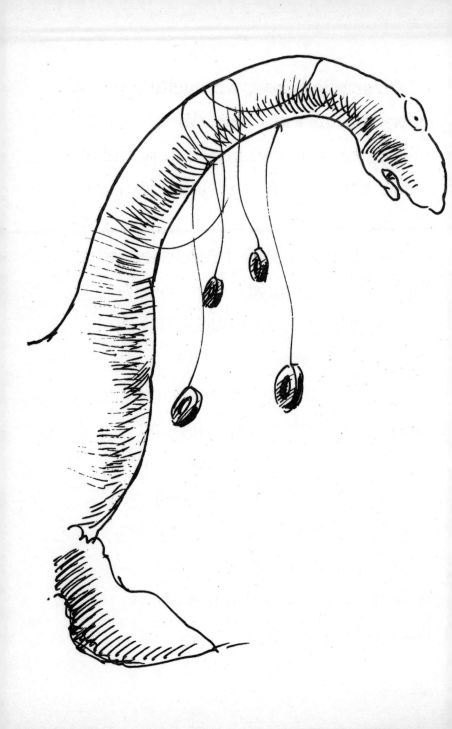

'It's getting away, it's getting away!'
howled Caroline. She did not blame
ART for this shambles, of course. She
blamed the idiots operating it.

But Mr Livingston was not beaten
yet. He sprinted for the yellow digger.

9

Nessie knew she was in big trouble.

Reptiles do not sweat, but they can certainly become over-excited; and if ever a reptile looked over-excited it was Nessie on the run.

Who on earth were those people! She was used to fainting tourists and polite scientists and sleepy old people wrapped up in rugs – she was not used to being ambushed by a wild horde of savage little beasts!

But she was almost safe now. The water lay not-too-far ahead and soon she would be out there swimming through the lough's gloomy deep. Then she saw the yellow monster

and her heart stood still.

The beast wasn't dead after all. Swaying to and fro, the monster snorted and clanked as it rolled towards her on the oddest pair of feet ever seen. However, those feet didn't bother her half as much as the creature's jaws. These jaws rose up and down, and they glinted horribly in the afternoon sun.

Oh doom, thought Nessie! It's the underwater zoo for me this time, all right. Or worse.

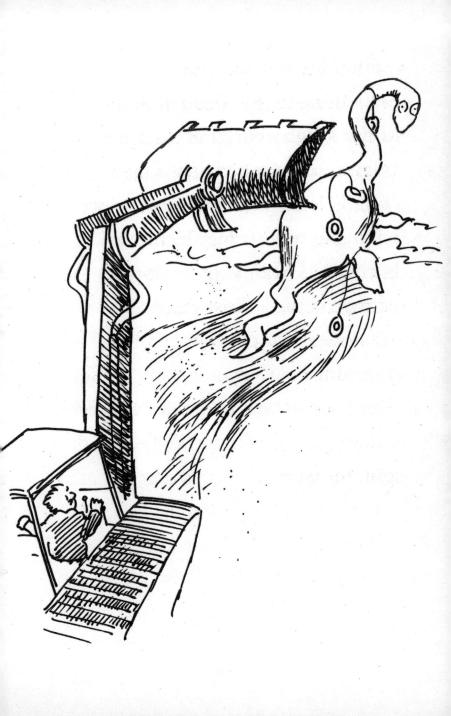

Then there came a terrifying roar.
Something broke through the waters
of the lough, reared up in a spray of
bright water, and charged up the
shore. Nessie could hardly believe
what she was seeing. Here was
boring old Nobby, of all things,
taking on the yellow beast!

The beast stopped in its tracks.
Would it now stay and fight a mighty
battle to the death? Nessie wondered.

Not at all. It whizzed right round
and ran away as fast as it could go.

And Nessie, with some
Ballymascullion rubber tyres, plunged
into the safe waters of the lough.

10

Noblett and Nessie sat with their heads above the water in the moonlight.

They weren't saying much to one another. Noblett sniffed the air as he often did, for the air in midsummer smelled sweet. How am I going to get rid of her? he was thinking.

Nessie's tail played with a rubber tyre. 'Hoots, Nobby, you saved my skin today, I must admit it. Of course you probably have a lot of those yellow things in Ireland and I suppose you know what cowards they are. But still, I'm very grateful.'

Nobby gazed at the moon

thoughtfully before replying.

'I don't think we've seen the last of the yellow monster. He'll be back with his friends. Oh no, we haven't seen the last of *him.*'

Nessie stopped playing with her tyre. 'His friends? How many of his friends?'

'Could be a hundred,' said Noblett. 'Could be more. There are a lot of them about these days. But perhaps we could barricade the front of the cave.'

'You mean they can go under the *water?*'

'They can go anywhere,' said Noblett. 'And they're strong. I've seen

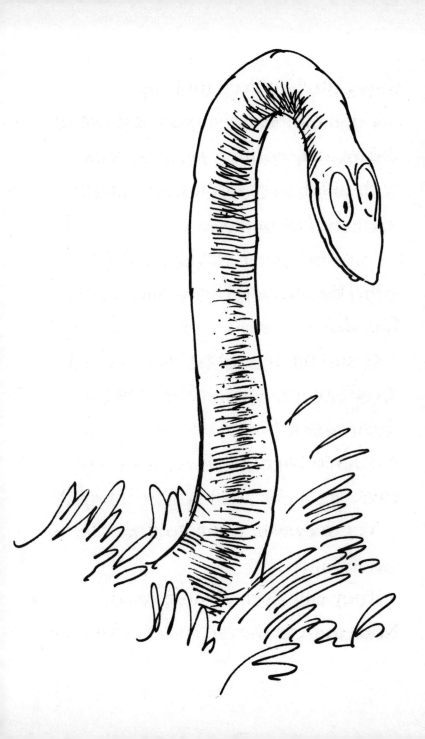

them dig holes right through mountains. We'll have to hide, of course – there'll be no more "fun".'

Now it was Nessie's turn to look thoughtfully at the moon. As she did so she may have imagined a mighty army of snorting yellow monsters on the march, for she suddenly stuck her tail through the rubber tyre she was keeping as a souvenir, and began to swim north.

'I have to go home now, Nobby,' she called out. 'Will you be all right?'

'If I'm careful,' said Noblett doubtfully.

'And will you ever visit me in Scotland?'

'Yes I will. Goodbye.'

If there's ever a drought in Ireland and Lough Neagh dries up, then I'll visit you, he was thinking as he dived down to his cave.

He knew what was going to happen now. They'd be after him in boats and canoes, they'd be swooping down from the sky in helicopters looking for the beast that scared windsurfers, chased sheep, chewed up clothes, stole bicycle sheds and beat up yellow diggers. And all thanks to his blasted cousin.

The best thing to do, he decided, was to look on the bright side of things. Perhaps the fuss would all die down, as it had died down a hundred years ago when Nessie ate that roof in Tyrone.

Time was the answer, and he had plenty of it. Nothing had happened that a few years' sleep wouldn't fix. He laid his great bulk down and closed his eyes, and tried not to think of the mess his garden would be in when he woke up again in the next century.

ALSO FROM THE O'BRIEN PRESS

THE *WOODLAND FRIENDS* SERIES,
WRITTEN AND ILLUSTRATED BY
DON CONROY

THE HEDGEHOG'S PRICKLY PROBLEM
Harry hedgehog joins the circus to find adventure, but then finds himself in a very prickly situation!

Paperback €5.07/STG£3.99

THE TIGER WHO WAS A ROARING SUCCESS
A large orange stranger turns up in the woodlands and causes havoc – and some fun!

Paperback €5.50/STG£3.99

THE BAT WHO WAS ALL IN A FLAP
A flying fox causes quite a stir in the woodland, but it's really Lenny the bat, far away from his home in Australia.

Paperback €5.50/STG£3.99

THE LEPRECHAUN WHO WISHED HE WASN'T

Siobhán Parkinson
Illustrated by Donald Teskey

Laurence is a leprechaun who has been small for 1,100 years and is SICK of it! He wants to be TALL. He wants to be cool. Then he meet Phoebe, a large girl who wants to be small. When she invites him to live in her house, Laurence is delighted. He starts wearing jeans and denim jackets and gets rid of the pointy hat. But there is one thing about leprechauns that you can't change – they are always up to mischief. And when Laurence decides to embark on a new career ... that's when the fun really starts!

Paperback €5.95/STG£4.50

Send for our full-colour catalogue